# STARRING Jules

## (THIRD GRADE DEBUT)

# BETH AIN

Illustrated by Anne Keenan Higgins

Scholastic Press / New York

★ ★ ★

Library of Congress Cataloging-in-Publication Data

Ain, Beth Levine, author.
Starring Jules (third grade debut) / Beth Ain ; illustrated by Anne Keenan Higgins.
pages cm. — (Starring Jules ; 4)
Summary: Jules is starting third grade, but her new teacher seems a little strange, she has to choose and research a famous person for the class wax museum project, and rehearsals for the sitcom she is in are harder than ever — especially since the TV show is about to air.
ISBN 978-0-545-44358-6
1. Child actors — Juvenile fiction. 2. Situation comedies (Television programs) — Juvenile fiction. 3. Elementary schools — Juvenile fiction. 4. Families — New York (State) — New York — Juvenile fiction. 5. New York (N.Y.) — Juvenile fiction.
[1. Actors and actresses — Fiction. 2. Television programs — Production and direction — Fiction. 3. Schools — Fiction. 4. Family life — Fiction. 5. New York (N.Y.) — Fiction.] I. Higgins, Anne Keenan, illustrator. II. Title. III. Title: Third grade debut.
PZ7.A277Sv 2014
813.6 — dc23
2013040179

Designed by Natalie C. Sousa

12 11 10 9 8 7 6 5 4 3 2 1          14 15 16 17 18 19/0

Printed in the U.S.A.                                          23
First printing, September 2014

For my
mom and dad
(as the producers)

# Lights! Camera! Action!

Read along as Jules Bloom's star
continues to rise:

*Starring Jules (as herself)*
*Starring Jules (in drama-rama)*
*Starring Jules (super-secret spy girl)*
*Starring Jules (third grade debut)*

Jules Bloom
in

LOOK AT US NOW!

# CONTENTS

street-fair leftovers,
babysitters with titles,
and other things that keep
you up at night

*How You Can Tell You Are Getting Old:*

1. The first day of third grade
   (and not second grade) is
   tomorrow.

2. One of the third-grade teachers used to be your numero uno best babysitter ever.

3. You got a different third-grade teacher.

4. Your little brother is going to kindergarten.

5. You have a job.

I put my notebook away and look out the window at the bright night. It is 8:06 p.m. and still light out and I am supposed to be going to sleep early. But there was a street fair today and the air still smells like lamb and peppers and roasted corn on the cob with *queso fresco*. Ay! How I miss my second-grade teacher, Ms. Leon, already!

Big Henry is snoring on the other side of the curtain and I wonder how he can sleep at a time like this. There is so much to think about. It took me almost an hour to lay out my first-day-of-school clothes all because it is going to be 300 degrees outside, which isn't corduroy weather at all. Instead, I have to wear shorts (rainbow) and a tank top (with a good-looking green apple on it), which is really more like camp clothing. It is very hard to get in a back-to-school mood without corduroy.

But Big Henry doesn't mind any of this. He is happy that he gets to wear the same mesh shorts he's worn every day since May. The only new thing he'll be wearing is a note card pinned to his shirt with his classroom and teacher written on it. I wish I had a note card to wear. If I did, it would say: *If this child is lost in a third-grade classroom, with a teacher who probably doesn't understand her, please return her to kindergarten, where she will color and learn her letters and where she will not be picked up after school by a car service that will take her to a TV studio in midtown. Instead, she will ride home on a scooter and eat snacks on the roof.*

I tiptoe past Big Henry's giant snoring self and out into the living room. My mom looks at me.

"Didn't we already do this once?" she asks.

★ 4 ★

"Do what?" I ask, even though I know what she means. We've said good night several times. I even interrupted my dad at his restaurant several times to say good night.

"Jules."

"Mommy."

"It's going to be a fun day tomorrow, and afterward, we'll go for ice cream," she says.

"No, that's the problem. After school is a *Look at Us Now!* rehearsal, so no first-day-of-school ice cream. I mean, it's not a problem, it's just a thing." I am careful not to say anything is a problem when it comes to being on a TV show. Otherwise, I will get the this-is-your-choice speech my mom or my dad makes every week or so.

"So we'll have ice cream after that," she says. "See? Problem solved. Go to bed." I sit down next to her. "What is it, Julesie? You have one more chance before I actually get angry."

"It's Mr. Santorini," I say. "Mister," I say again. "I've never had a boy teacher before and I heard he's really weird and gives tons of homework."

"He's not a boy teacher, Jules. He's a man, and he isn't weird. He's quirky. There's a difference," my mom says. "And just because people say something about him doesn't mean it's true. You need to see for yourself. Besides, his name is the same as a beautiful Greek island with turquoise water and white-sand beaches and all the lamb and peppers you like so much at street fairs. Picture that when you meet him tomorrow."

"I just wish I could have had Avery," I say.

"That wouldn't have been fair and you know it. She's like family. And don't forget, Jules. At school, she's Ms. Kaplan."

I snort at this. How am I supposed to call a girl who does yoga headstands on my bed while blasting rap music Ms. Kaplan?

"Anyway," my mom says, "at least they kept the four of you together."

By "the four of you," my mom means Elinor, my best friend forever whose beautiful British accent makes everything better every day; Charlotte, my ex–best friend forever, who acts like a gigantic snob most of the time but who sometimes is nice by accident; Teddy Meant-to-Be Lichtenstein, who still calls me by my Periodic Table of Elements name, and who will definitely find a whole bunch of new ways to bump into me every day; and me. The lucky ones who did not get Mr. Looks-Like-Lamb-and-Peppers Santorini are Abby and Brynn, who will be spending their time with a certain yoga-posing teacher who will probably have pizza parties at least once a week. Or maybe tapas parties. Tapas are small plates of food. Avery loves tapas.

"Right," I say to my mom. "The four of us."

"Bed, Jules."

"What time is it?" I ask.

"8:20," she says.

"What time exactly?" I ask. The exact time is important.

"8:19."

"Perfect."

"Why?"

"Because that gives me eleven minutes to fall asleep at an even number."

My mom shakes her head and shoos me away. I stop to look at my brother, who is asleep with his hands behind his head. Suddenly, he opens his eyes for one second, yells "I WANT LEMONADE!" at the top of his lungs, and closes his eyes again.

I run over and hop onto my bed and laugh hysterically into my pillow. He was probably dreaming about the lemonade lady at the street fair. He was so thirsty after bouncing on the giant bouncers he whined about lemonade until we finally got to the lady who sings her lemonade jingle all day so you can find her easily. I was thinking *she* should be on TV with that voice and that jingle, and not me with my boring old fizzy-milk jingle.

I look out the window again. Finally the sky is getting dark and my clock says 8:24. Six minutes left to fall asleep. Six minutes until second grade is officially over and I am a third grader with a kindergartner

brother, a third grader with a brand-new teacher who probably doesn't like rap music, a third grader with a job as the sassy little sister on a TV show that probably everyone in the world will watch.

I never see 8:30 on the clock, which means — and this is a bad thing — I must fall asleep at a very odd time.

## gooey omelets, firm handshakes, and invisible lies

Big Henry is up at the crack of dawn and all
I can do is put my pillow over my head and
hope he doesn't come jump on me. I hear
him whisper-yell my name —

"Jules!"

He has worked very hard on getting rid of

his lisp all summer long and now I feel a little bit sad that it is mostly gone, especially when he says my name. I don't respond to him, though, because I am not ready for the day. I hear him run down the hall toward my parents and our first-day-of-school breakfast selection.

I want to go back to sleep for a few more minutes, but I can't close my eyes. I am picturing a breakfast buffet of yogurt parfaits, and waffles with cream, and sliced tomatoes piled high with giant slices of mozzarella cheese, like the ones they have at Mother's Day celebrations at fancy restaurants. I get up and walk toward the kitchen.

"Hey, where's my tomatoes and cheese?" I ask.

"I'm sorry, Julesie," my dad says. "I couldn't get to the place with the good mozzarella, so today omelets will have to do."

"Omelets are gross," I say.

"Jules!" my mom says now. "How about you try that again?"

"Omelets are a little bit gross?" I ask. "Like, gross in the best possible cheese-oozing-out-of-the-sides kind of way?"

My mom narrows her eyes at me. "I'm assuming you're nervous about the first day, but try and be positive. It's Henry's first day, too, you know."

"Kindergarten!" he yells, and egg flies out of his mouth and halfway across the kitchen in celebration. I feel like I'm going to throw up at this — the only thing grosser than cheese oozing out of an omelet is egg bits flying out of your little brother's mouth.

"Jules," my dad says, "to make it up to you, I'll put tomatoes inside your omelet. The eggs will be good for your brain. They make you think." My dad has a way of turning every food into something very important. If I tried to keep a list of things he says about food, it would go on and on and on until forever, starting with:

1. "Only eat things fresh from local organic farms."

2. "The darker the chocolate the better." (Even if it's so dark it stops tasting like chocolate

and starts tasting like the
wood chips under the swings in
Central Park.)

3. "The sweet potato is a real gem
   of a tuber." (Tuber is a very
   grown-up, organic-chef word
   for a vegetable that grows
   underground. I plan to impress
   my new teacher with this word.)

Then there would be about thirty gazil-
lion more things on the list about tart
cherries and coconut milk and the sleep
benefits of kiwi fruit and pumpkin seeds. And
then the list would end one day a long, long
time from now, with my father's favorite

reason why people should eat this way: "So we can all live to be 350 years old and take walks down Broadway arm in arm with our great-great-great-great-grandchildren."

I think it would be okay to live only until maybe 225 and occasionally eat some milk chocolate, but I never say that to him. I just smile and eat kale-and-tomato omelets.

After we get all dressed up in our first-day-of-school clothes, we kiss my dad good-bye and head downstairs in the elevator. In the lobby, Joe the doorman high-fives us and Big Henry shows off.

"Let's see those karate-chopping break-dance moves," Joe says. He loves Big Henry. Everybody does. And it's because if someone asks Big Henry to do his karate-chopping break-dance moves, he just starts doing it, with no music or anything, and with a backpack filled with brand-new school supplies on his back.

If someone asks me to show off my moves — moves like, I don't know, thinking too much or maybe singing on a countertop on a TV show — I always find a leg to hold on to like I'm still in nursery school. I think my third-grade resolution is to one day show off my moves just like Big Henry does, smack in the middle of everything.

"An apple for the teacher — I like it, Jules," Joe says to me when Big Henry's dance show is over.

I smile at him and wave, but I don't know what he's talking about. "Your shirt," my mom says to me once we're on the street. "People always say you should bring an apple for the teacher, so I guess that's what Joe thought you were doing by wearing that shirt."

"It wasn't," I say. "But will that make him like me?"

"He'll like you because you're you, Jules. Apple or no apple."

I don't really believe her so I'm very glad I have the apple just in case.

*Some things happen when we get to school:*

1. Big Henry doesn't cry.

2. He doesn't hold on extra tight to my mom's hand and beg her not to leave.

3. He doesn't ask her to double-check to make sure she has packed the right three-ring binder, the 1 1/2-inch one that was listed on the kindergarten school supplies list they sent home with classroom assignments.

4. When my mom pulls him back to her for one last hug, he wiggles out of it and says, "Okay, okay, I have to go!"

Mom and I just stand there staring at him as he walks through the very same doors that have practically scared the breakfast out of me every single first day of school for the last three years, like it's nothing.

"Don't be sad, Julesie," my mom says now.

"I'm not," I lie.

"You wanted to walk him into Ms. Kim's room, right? You wanted to be the big kid on the block walking your little brother in there and giving your old kindergarten teacher a hug, right?"

"I guess," I say, and I shrug. I still hate it when I shrug. I wish I could get my body to forget how to shrug. "Well, gotta go," I say.

"No hug?" she says. "You don't have to show off for Big Henry. I'll tell him you didn't need a hug, either."

I hug her tight. "That would be a lie," I say.

"A teeny-tiny white lie," she says.

"Almost invisible," I say.

"I can live with it," she says.

I'm smiling and walking through the door when my mom says, "Remember it's not going to be a perfect day." I look around to make sure no one heard her say that, and even though no one does, my face burns up anyway. I walk inside and find my way to Mr. Santorini's third-grade classroom, crossing everything but my eyes hoping he doesn't hate me.

I walk in and something strange is going on. No one else is in the room. Not even the teacher. Not even Charlotte, who is always first to everything. I feel the butterflies rev up in my belly and I try to calm them by finding my cubby and unpacking my backpack. The best part of arriving for the first day of school is pulling out of your brand-new rainbow-striped backpack the perfect black-and-white marble notebook and a box of pointy, sharpened pencils, ready for freewriting.

"Oh, hello there!" I hear behind me, and I turn around to see Mr. Santorini and a whole pack of kids filing in behind him. I feel like there's a spotlight shining on me. And not in a good way.

"Hi," I say quietly, making sure not to open my mouth so wide that little diced omelet tomatoes come flying out.

"I grabbed the early birds who were here for a quick run down the hall to get some nervous first-day energy out." Then he turns back to the small group and says, "Ten-hut!" and clicks his shoes together so loud my belly drops to my feet. My friends look at each other. "We'll get to that later, sailors."

I feel my mouth hanging open a little and close it quickly. Early birds? A quick run in the hallway? Sailors? This Mr. Santorini feels like a character on *Look at Us Now!* and not like a real-life teacher at all.

"Jules!" Elinor breaks the weird silence and comes over to me. "Look, we're sitting next to each other!"

"Ah! Bloom, Jules," Mr. Santorini says, looking at a list he's holding in his hand. He walks over to me with his hand out. "Very nice to meet you." When I look at him closely, I realize he looks a little bit like Captain von Trapp from *The Sound of Music*, if Captain von Trapp would ever wear a Hawaiian shirt, that is. I'm just hoping he doesn't have a whistle.

I put my hand out and let him shake it. "Hmmm," he says. "Let's try that again. This time when I shake, shake back, sailor." I know what he means about the shake because this is how Colby Kingston, my

agent, shakes hands. I just didn't know it
was okay to shake a teacher's hand this way.
I also don't know why he's calling me "sailor."

"Very nice to meet you," Mr. Santorini
says again.

I grab on and shake firmly this time. I also stand up a little straighter and clear my throat. I feel like my TV character, Sylvie, would handle all of this better than I am handling it, and I also think that this quirky Mr. Santorini would like Sylvie, my sit-com character, better than Jules Bloom, or Bloom, Jules — worm-digging Upper West Sider.

"Likewise," I say with gusto — *gusto* is a script word — shaking his hand hard. Sylvie always says things like "likewise," and I always wonder who would actually say something like this in real life, but I realize now that my new third-grade teacher, who calls people "sailor" and says last names first, is definitely someone who says "likewise."

"Okay, then," he says, and turns back to the others, who have started making their way to their seats.

"Where's Charlotte?" I ask Elinor when we sit down. She shrugs at this, which makes me happy because even my completely cool and calm very best friend shrugs sometimes. Even she talks with her shoulders when she doesn't know what else to say.

"She's coming late," Teddy says.

"Lichtenstein, Theodore," Mr. Santorini says.

I snort into my hand at this as Mr. Santorini shows Teddy to his seat.

"Hi, Teddy," Elinor says when Teddy falls into the chair next to hers, and I realize I'm glad Teddy and I are separated by a whole person. "How do you know she'll be late?"

"Teddy always knows everything," I say. And he does. He's like the guy on the radio show that wakes me up in the morning. He knows the weather, the news, and whatever happened on TV last night. And he apparently knows that Charlotte Stinkytown Pinkerton, former best friend, and current not-as-terrible-as-I-thought sort-of friend, is going to be late for the first day of third grade. "So why is she late? Charlotte's never been late for anything, and especially not the first day of school."

"I saw her last night at the diner and she said she had an appointment they can't change. That's all I know," Teddy says.

Elinor and I look at each other. Very suspicious. Who has an appointment on the first day of school?

At last, Mr. Santorini clears his throat and we all quiet down. "Welcome to third grade," he says. "Third grade is run like a tight ship, sailors. We will respect each other, be well behaved, and we will be curious and brave. This ship is sailing to wonderful, far-off places where fiction and facts meet; where every piece of writing will have a beginning, a middle, and end; where we will multiply and divide; and where we will get to know each other and some new people, too, through biographies . . ."

I can hardly believe how much Mr. Santorini is talking and how much he seems like an actor in a movie about a sea captain who has been punished by having to teach a bunch of third graders in New York City. A sea captain who thought a Hawaiian shirt would be a good way to win us over. He *must* be an actor. I'm just waiting for the jazz hands to prove it.

". . . and where we will create our very own wax museum!" I snap out of the imaginary sea-captain movie when he says "wax museum." *Wax museum*, I think, smiling. These are two words that separately sound boring, but together they sound magical. A magical museum of wax — I don't know what it means. All I know is it sounds way better than fractions!

Before I can hear more, the door opens

and there she is. Charlotte Stinkytown Pinkerton.

"Pinkerton, Charlotte," Mr. Santorini says, looking at his class list again. I'm trying so hard not to laugh that my whole body is shaking. The thing is, I don't know if Mr. Santorini thinks he's being funny, and the worst thing you can do is laugh at someone when they are being serious. I know this firsthand because my parents sometimes laugh when they think I am kidding and it is not funny to me at all.

But all of a sudden I notice something and I forget all about the last-names-first thing: Stinkytown is making the biggest entrance of her life and I feel like I might explode. I knew if she was going to be late

for the first day of third grade there was going to be a very big reason, and is there ever. Stinkytown, Charlotte, is wearing glasses.

Now that laughing feeling is gone and all I feel is something tightening up in the middle of my stomach right behind the apple on my shirt, right where that omelet probably was, which makes me wonder if all that gooey cheese can tie itself into a knot this long after you've chewed it.

Elinor hits me on the arm right then because:

1. Elinor is my very best friend in the whole world.

2. Some things only your very best friend in the whole world knows about you.

3. My best friend in the whole world knows that more than anything else in the world, more than being an actress even, the only thing I really want and probably won't ever get, is glasses.

TAKE THREE

## recess calisthenics, heavy squinting, and other extracurricular activities

It takes me all morning to stop staring at Charlotte's glasses. Sometimes you forget to really look at your friends, which means you forget that they are pretty or that they have freckles or crooked teeth because you're busy just being with them. But now I know where every last freckle on Charlotte's face is, and that is because they are mostly on her nose — the same nose where her pink-with-polka-dots glasses sit. The glasses are perfect. I might have even chosen them myself if they didn't have turquoise ones. Do they have turquoise glasses? They must. They have pink-with-polka-dots glasses. I never even thought about all the glasses possibilities, but now I can't think of anything else.

"So, eat a healthy lunch and do your jumping jacks at recess, sailors," Mr. Santorini is saying. "Get all that physical energy out and come back ready to focus on fractions. We don't want any yellows or reds on the first day!"

My new third-grade teacher — the one who calls us sailors and who swears by morning jogs in the hallway and jumping jacks at recess — also believes in behavior charts. This means that if you do one little thing wrong, you get your color changed from green to yellow, and if that thing you do gets worse, or if you do something else that's bad, then you go to red — RED — and red means a call home. But what is the very bad thing that turns a person red? I don't know. And I don't want to ask because what if I raise my hand at the exact wrong time and THAT is the very bad thing that turns me red? Between staring at Charlotte's face and the chart on the wall, my eyes feel almost crossed by the time lunch finally comes.

It is a salad bar day, which only adds to my problems. I usually love salad bar because I can pile up black olives on my plate and shredded cheese and crunchy lettuce and ranch dressing, but today having to take all my own food and balance it on my tray makes me extra tired. *Why can't I ever feel this tired at bedtime?*

Finally I make it to our table, and Elinor and I sit together watching Charlotte eat the cucumber-and-avocado sushi roll her mother bought her as a first-day-of-school treat.

"Can you see me now?" Teddy asks Charlotte.

"I could always see you," Charlotte says. "I can just see you better. I don't have to squint."

I feel myself squinting when she says the word *squint*, and I think maybe I should ask my mom for a doctor's appointment when I get home. Maybe I do need glasses.

"How did you know you needed them?" Elinor asks.

"I don't know. I kept rubbing my eyes at camp. I thought it was allergies. I thought I couldn't see the stage because there was pollen in my eyes or something. Then we went to the movies a couple of days ago and when the title was up on the screen I realized it looked blurry, too. I had to squint to see clearly. Then my mom rushed to make an appointment and we found out I needed glasses. Today was the soonest we could pick them up, so that's why I was late. My mom didn't want me to start third grade with blurry vision."

*And so you could make an entrance,* I think to myself. *You and your perfect pink polka-dot glasses.* But I don't say this out loud. I just listen to everyone giving Charlotte all kinds of attention and I stare at my black olives, suddenly wishing they were sushi rolls instead. I do not like wishing for glasses and sushi rolls on the first day of school. I like thinking about Ms. Leon's accent and freewriting. I feel my head start to pound and I definitely think I might need that doctor's appointment.

Somehow I make it through a very sweaty recess and a very sweaty rest of the school day and never once do I run into Big Henry and never once do I run into Avery — I mean, Ms. Kaplan — and it feels like the whole first day of school is going on around me and that I am missing it. I pray that Mr. Santorini will tell us about the wax museum but he never does, and I don't want to ask about it since I'm afraid of getting a yellow card for being impatient or something. I decide to be patient. I'm patient all the way to dismissal, when I find my mom in a hurry.

"How was it, Julesie?" I feel so many feelings I can't answer her, so I do something I know she doesn't like. I bump my body into

hers a little too hard and hope she doesn't ask me any more questions. She ignores me and I listen as she chitchats with everyone she hasn't seen all summer long. My mom is very good at talking to other people nicely even when I know she's not happy with me. I can tell because her voice gets a little bit louder and she laughs too hard at nothing. Things get worse when Big Henry comes running out holding Ms. Kim's hand. He looks so happy and so cute with his backpack and his smile. I feel like bumping into him a little too hard, too.

"Hank!" my mom yells, and he comes flying into her arms and wraps his legs around her and they hug each other super tight. Ms. Kim gives my mom a thumbs-up and says "Great day!" before delivering all the other kindergartners to their parents.

"Big Henry is lucky," I say as we walk. It's hard for me to even get a word in since Big Henry is talking and talking and talking and talking.

"Why?" he asks.

"Why?" I say, mocking his little voice.

"Jules," my mom says calmly. Too calmly. I look at the ground. "Jules," she says again. "I told you the day would not be perfect."

"You did not say it would be horrible," I say.

"I didn't know it would be," she says. "And I am sorry it was horrible, but it is not okay to push me and it is not okay to mock Big Henry. Clear?"

"Clear," I say.

"Let's take some deep breaths in the car," she says.

"Are we going to sitcom practice now?" Big Henry asks. He talks about the sitcom like it's soccer practice. He also says the word *sitcom* about three hundred times a day, which was funny when it started but now it hurts my ears.

We are waiting on the corner for a car service, which is like a taxi except you can reserve it and it isn't yellow and it doesn't have a TV that shows you the weather forecast. This is how we will be getting to the studio every day while we rehearse and tape the sitcom *Look at Us Now!*, where I play a girl named Sylvie who does all kinds of things I would never do, including singing on countertops.

I spent a lot of my summer rehearsing and taping the show and now, in two weeks, on a Sunday night, the first episode is going to air on television and my parents are going to have a party at my dad's restaurant, BLOOM. We only have a few more episodes to go, but now that school has started, it means I'll be missing some days when we tape, which means A LOT of extra work, but I don't care. I love this TV show. I love it way more than filming a spy movie in another country where everyone speaks another language and where I had to turn eight without my dad or Elinor there to blow out candles with me. Besides, after filming a movie with teenage megastar Emma Saxony, who was the main star of *The Spy in the Attic* and who is not nearly as pretty inside as she is outside, even, I think, homework — loads and loads of homework — will be fun.

We hop into the car and I feel better already, thinking about going back to the set. I even feel like making a list!

*Reasons Why I Will Be Happy for the Rest of the Day:*

1. There will be a babysitter on set for Big Henry, so he can go be all happy about kindergarten somewhere else.

2. There will be air conditioning from here on out.

3. The first day of third grade is over.

When we arrive, no matter how happy I am, I get butterflies. Butterflies and acting go together for me. Like chocolate and mint. My mom delivers Big Henry to the babysitter and I can still hear his voice talking as she leads him down a hallway and far, far away. I can STILL hear his voice in my head after he is long gone. "Ms. Kim" this, and "choice time" that, and "recess" this . . . I can't imagine having that much to say about third grade already.

"Sylvie, darlin'!" I hear my sitcom name and smile. My big sister has arrived.

I smile big at Jordana, whose sitcom name is Sydney. She has the thickest Southern accent I've ever heard, except when she's being Sydney, then she sounds just like everyone I know in real life and I think this is what makes her a very good actress. "*Very talented*," Colby Kingston always says about the kids on *Look at Us Now!*

"How was the first day, y'all?" she asks while looking at her phone. She is also talented at doing a lot of things at once, which according to my mom is something all teenagers are good at. Jordana used to make me nervous with all of her teenager-y ways, but then she started teaching me things and making me laugh when I was anxious, and now I love her, like a real-life sister.

"Maybe Jules will tell *you*, Jordana," my mom says. "Might be a case only a sitcom big sister can solve."

"Or a sitcom big brother," John McCarthy, formerly the Swish Mouthwash boy, now my sitcom older brother, says. "This is why you gotta give up on school and get a tutor."

"Ahem!" my mom says, fake-clearing her throat. "Not happening, McCarthy."

My mom thinks John McCarthy is very hilarious. They always talk to each other like grown-ups, which makes me picture them at a café sipping tall icy drinks and talking about the news. If someone told me last year when I was in the waiting room of the Swish Mouthwash auditions, staring at the boy in the short-sleeve buttoned-up

★ 52 ★

shirt and bow tie, KNOWING that he would be the Swish kid and that I would definitely not be — well, if someone told me the Swish boy and I would one day soon be sitcom siblings and that my mom and the Swish boy would be sharing imaginary tall icy drinks, I would have squinted so hard at that person, they definitely would have thought I needed glasses. But here we are. Look at us now.

TAKE FOUR

## small plates, dummy lessons, and rotten surprises

"Make a list for me, Jules. Tell me all about the pain and suffering of third grade in list form. Go!" Jordana says.

It's already been one whole week since meeting my brand-new third-grade sea captain — I mean, teacher — and a week since staring Charlotte and her glasses in the freckly face. A week since we were told there would be something called a wax museum, and a week since we were introduced to the behavior chart that keeps my mouth zipped up tighter than ever.

"I can't," I say.

"Can't or won't?" Jordana asks.

"Can't," I say. "I cannot make a list. We don't even have freewriting time in third grade. I haven't made a list in days! I bet Avery's class has freewriting."

"You think everything is better over there in Avery's room, huh?"

"It *is* better," I say. "I know it is. Brynn

and Abby told us at recess that they are going to have a tapas party if everyone stays green all week. Tapas!"

"That sounds very weird."

"It *is* weird," I say. "That's why I love it."

"Does Mr. Santorini have parties?" she asks. "He wears Hawaiian shirts."

"No way, José. He thinks kids get too many rewards. We should be good because we are supposed to be good. And that's that." I say this and don't realize that I am imitating him. Now I picture

myself wearing a Hawaiian shirt and doing jumping jacks.

"Hmmm," Jordana says. "He's a tough cookie. I'll have to think about that one. And what's happening on the glasses front?"

"Well, I have a doctor's appointment tomorrow because Mom realized she never made me an eight-year-old checkup, so fingers crossed!" I say.

"Jules, your vision is perfect," she says. "You wouldn't be able to read the teleprompter if it weren't."

"We'll see about that," I say, squinting.

We get back to rehearsal and right away I forget all about school and glasses and behavior charts. I realize how happy I am to fit in here after feeling very out of place all day long.

When I play Sylvie, I get to do things I would never do in real life. I get to sing at the top of my lungs, I get to talk to older kids like John McCarthy and Jordana in a way that I would never, ever talk to older kids if I ever met them in real life. In real life, I get nervous when one of the older kids in my building asks me something in the elevator. They say things like "Cute backpack." And it would be really easy for me to say "Thanks," but I just get all hot in the face and my mom always says "What do you say?" to me like I'm three years old.

If Sylvie were in the same exact situation, she would say, *"I was deciding between rainbow and peace signs and went with rain-bow, since peace signs seemed a little last year to me.*" Then everyone would laugh and the director would say "*Cut,*" and we'd all get out of the fake elevator and get a drink of water. But as Jules, I always get out of the elevator feeling bad that I don't know how to talk to people when I don't have a script.

This week's episode of *Look at Us Now!* is about Spencer having a crush on a girl who wants to try out for the same reality show that made Mr. and Mrs. Summers so famous. The whole idea of our show is that the Summers family used to live a regular life in a regular apartment until the parents struck it rich on a big-time reality TV show.

So the thing is, even though I always have to say a lot of funny things and make a lot of funny faces when I play Sylvie, in this episode I have to do some very crazy things with my body. The director tells me this is called "physical comedy," which I already know because usually people tell me I'm good at it! My mom always says this is the kind of comedy that makes kids laugh the hardest. But this is different. This isn't acting like a funny person. This is acting like a funny doll! In this scene, John's character, Spencer, makes Sylvie come with him to his crush's audition, and they audition together as a ventriloquist and his puppet, called . . . a dummy! Sylvie is the dummy and I'm having a LOT of trouble understanding how to not act like a person. The script says, "Sylvie opens and closes her mouth like a wooden dummy, with big wide eyes, and she turns her head side to side and she says her jokes." I concentrate really hard on what everyone tells me at the table read, but I just end up feeling silly acting like a dummy.

I think back to sliding down that giant mudslide in Canada when we filmed *The*

*Spy in the Attic*, and how nervous I was and how glad I was when I did it without a stunt double, and I don't know why this feels harder than that.

We work on this for a while and no matter how many times we do it, something is keeping me from playing the scene the way I know I should. I'm afraid of really going for it because what if it isn't funny? What if I am horribly embarrassed in front of everyone? It's the same feeling that behavior chart gives me — the what-if feeling.

The director says it will be easier when the makeup is on and I look like an actual dummy. That's what he says to me and I have gone from feeling very in place to very out of place. I spend the last half hour of rehearsal wanting to go home, which is the OPPOSITE of how I usually feel when I'm here. Anyway, when I hear "That's a wrap!" I am very relieved. No one is happy with my read-through. Even my mom seems frustrated, and she's not one of the moms who even cares if I act or not, but now she seems mad the way John McCarthy's mom does if he looks like he's having too much fun. My mom shakes her head at me and apologizes to the director, and suddenly I am very happy that there is no behavior chart for acting because I think I would have gotten a yellow for sure.

We pick up Big Henry from the babysitter and we have to practically drag him home by his arm, he's so tired. Finally my mom just picks him up, slinging his backpack over her shoulder.

"Can you hold me instead?" I ask.

"Hold *you*?" she asks.

"Please?" I ask.

"Jules, I think you need to walk off your frustration, and anyway, I can hardly hold this guy," she says. I know I should grab his backpack from her and be helpful but I think if she's going to choose one of us to carry and the one she chooses is not me, then I am going to punish her by not carrying his backpack. It's probably not even heavy anyway since he eats everything in his lunch and has exactly one worksheet — *Crazy About C!* — in his homework folder.

"I'm soooo tired!" Big Henry moans as my mom hoists him up farther onto her.

"Can I have a playdate during sitcom practice tomorrow?" he asks. His voice is making me feel itchy.

"Can *I* have a playdate instead of sitcom practice?" I ask, knowing that the answer will be no and knowing that even *asking* this question is going to drive my mom crazy.

She just looks at me. "Neither one of you needs a playdate for tomorrow's sitcom practice because tomorrow we are going for Jules's checkup. Problem solved!" Her voice makes it sound like the problem isn't solved at all, but I remember to get back to squinting so I am good and ready for my eye exam.

When we finally get home, I open up my folder while my mom makes dinner. All I want is one of my dad's homemade meatballs and a whole pile of spaghetti, but my mom is going to give me plain pasta and broccoli, I just know it. And that means Ugly Otis will get a very nutritious meal and I will go to bed thinking about ground-up steak.

I hear another giant moan come out of Big Henry, and this time it is because he has homework to do. He is stuck on reading the word *cat*. CAT! I am sitting here doing about a hundred math problems and I still have to memorize my multiplication tables AND read for thirty whole minutes. I kick him under the table.

"HEY!" he yells. Now I am really mad because now my mom is going to get mad at me and it's all because of Big Henry I-Have-NOTHING-to-Moan-About Bloom.

My mom turns around and stares at us from the stove. She asks a question with her eyebrows, and the answer is, "Jules kicked me!"

"He was whining!" I yell. "And I have to concentrate."

"Go concentrate in your room," she says. "Now. And take an apple with you. You're probably hungry and tired. Dinner will be ready in fifteen minutes. And stop squinting!" she yells. "You're going to need glasses if you keep that up."

I smile the whole way to my room. *Yes!* But the feeling goes away quickly because there is nothing worse than having to eat an apple when what you really want is a meatball. I plop down on my floor and take one bite before I put it carefully on the other side of our room-divider curtain. Now the once-bitten apple will live on Big Henry's side of the room and he will have to do something about it at bedtime. I do all my work and it feels like it is going to be midnight before I finish, which doesn't even count all the time I spend thinking about that behavior chart and Charlotte's glasses and when, when, when Mr. Santorini will tell us what the wax museum is.

I hear my mom raising her voice trying to get Hank to make his Cs a little nicer, and I wish life was kindergarten-simple again. I make really good Cs.

TAKE FIVE

## Florida calling, waxing poetic, and good strong library smells

I wake up in a better mood because Grandma Gilda calls first thing and Big Henry brings her to me under my covers.

"Eddie," she says into my ear.

"George," I say back. Ever since I came

up with the idea to call her George, the nickname has stuck. It's our thing.

"I'm calling with some morning positive affirmations," she says. Positive affirmations are Grandma Gilda's thing. "Today is going to be a great third-grade day," she says.

"Today is going to be a great third-grade day," I say, yawning.

"Today is going to be a great *Look at Us Now!* day," she says.

"Today is going to be a great *Look at Us Now!* day," I say.

"Today I will change my name to Pickle," she says.

"Today I will change my name to . . ." I stop. "HEY!" I shout.

Then I hear Big Henry outside of my covers. He is hysterically laughing. I throw off the covers and look at my brother.

"I said it. I said I was going to change my name to Pickle," he says. Then he sits down on the floor and rolls around in fake laughter.

"You got Big Henry," I tell Grandma Gilda. "But you did not get me, George."

"Almost, Eddie. Al-most," she says.

"You are too far away," I say. "Next time you try to play a trick on me, come to New York City and do it."

"Okey doke!" she says.

When I come into the kitchen my dad is getting a lick from Ugly Otis. "Why does Ugly Otis have broccoli breath?" he asks me.

"Why don't you go on a big-time reality cooking show?" I say back. This is a good distraction.

"You're changing the subject," he says, smiling. I wish I could reverse the days so this part happens last. It would be so much better if my dad could help me with multiplication and shine his bright smile on us when the sun is going down and I have no more energy. But now that BLOOM is open, I only see him in the morning because he spends every night at work.

"Well, why don't you?" I ask. "We could be like the Summers family if you win!"

"Yeah!" Big Henry says, and his voice is still annoying to me even this morning after all that sleep.

"Do you really want to be like the Summers family?" he asks. "Aren't the parents never, ever home?"

"Uncle Ike is home. He takes care of them," Big Henry says. Big Henry is a *Look at Us Now!* expert.

"I have an idea," I say. "Uncle Michael could take care of us!"

"Yeah!" Hank cheers. Uncle Michael is like a rock star. He shows up with his guitar and we sing and dance and make videos on his computer and he pushes us way too high on the swing at Hippo Playground and he makes you feel like you're on vacation when you haven't even gone anywhere different.

"Oh, right," my mom says. "I'd like to see that. You'd be eating takeout every night and playing video games till three a.m."

"That's why it would be fun," I say.

"And that's why Daddy isn't trying out for any big-time TV cooking shows," my mom says.

"And also because I have a restaurant to run. Remember?" my dad asks. "Some people don't just go on TV and become stars, Jules Bloom. Some people do things the old-fashioned way."

"Did you have phones in the old-fashioned time?" Hank asks.

"Did you have roads in the old-fashioned

time?" I ask, squinting. I'm trying to squint as much as possible before today's doctor's appointment. My dad shakes his spatula at us and Big Henry and I crack up. George's positive affirmations are working already!

Outside, it is raining, but I don't get mad. At least it isn't hot and sticky, for once. *It is going to be a great third-grade day,* I think. We hustle across Broadway and my foot lands smack in the middle of slimy sidewalk-corner water. *It is going to be a great third-grade day,* I think again. Then my mom's umbrella turns inside out, and we miss the bus by about one half of a second. I look at my mom and her broken umbrella and her wet self and I think that she is going to explode. Since I am the one who

usually explodes and she is the one who puts me back together, I decide to help. "Today I will change my name to Pickle," I say.

My mom just looks at me like I'm nutso and smiles. "Thanks, Pickle," she says. And just like that, another bus arrives.

Today, Mr. Santorini tells us to take our seats extra quick. Then he hands out bandanas to everyone. "Line up at the door and tie 'em over your eyes, sailors! No jumping jacks this morning. No jogging, either. Today's for something different." I think it's funny that he doesn't think jumping jacks and jogging aren't something different, but I don't think about that for too long.

Elinor and I look at each other before we tie our bandanas on. She mouths *What on earth?* to me and I smile-squint big at her. We put them on and we are then led in a line down the hallway, hands on each other's shoulders, to a dark room. I know it's dark because the lights are off, not because of a blackout or something, but my legs shake anyway. I can't teach my legs not to shake when it gets dark all of a sudden. They don't know something amazing is about to happen. Something amazing like music in the dark at school. A voice tells us to take off our bandanas. When we do, we're in the cafetorium, and there is Avery on the stage and all these flashing lights and she is dressed up with sunglasses, leading all three third-grade teachers in a rap.

And the rap goes like this:

This is the moment you are waiting
 for. . . .
Want to be Roosevelt, El-ea-nor?
Do you like hockey and bas-ket-ball?
Do you wanna be a scientist like Jane
 Goodall?
Maybe you are more of an acting type,
Or maybe Wilbur or Orville Wright?!

*Do you like politics or history?*
*Want to learn about John F. Kennedy?*
*Want to see what made Julie Andrews*
   *sing,*
*Or everything about Dr. Martin Luther*
   *King?*
*Whoever it is, whatever you be-a*
*We can't wait to see who plays*
*Sacagawea, Sac-Sac-a-ga-wea!*
*So we'll start today because you have to*
   *meet 'em.*
*Three weeks to go until the wax*
   *mu-se-um!*

We all cheer our heads off, and clap and
hoot and holler and something tells me
this rap thing was all Avery's idea. Rap

and tapas. That's just her thing. I feel the best kind of butterflies in my stomach — not the nervous, going-to-throw-up kind, but the excited, how-did-I-ever-live-before-this-news kind. When we finally settle down, we are told that each class will get a special library session today to look at biographies and decide who we will want to be in the wax museum project. Then we will research every little thing about the person we choose and we will write reports on them and make a timeline and then — and this is the BEST part of all — on the day of the wax museum, we get to dress up like them and stand in a room like a real wax museum! I don't even know what a real wax museum is, but it sounds AMAZING

and interesting and it is my absolute favorite thing that has ever happened since the
second-grade hoedown.

And now I finally have some exciting
things to write about this school year that
have nothing to do with jumping jacks or
glasses. And the best news is, I feel like writing a list! I can't wait to tell Jordana.

1. I love blindfolds.

2. I love the wax museum.

3. I love third grade.

On our way back to the classroom, I
finally see Avery — er, Ms. Kaplan — in

the hallway, and she sticks out her tongue at me when no one is looking. I stick mine out VERY quickly and stick it back in again. Then we go back to being our school-time selves.

I think I spend the entire next forty-five minutes bouncing my knee because that is how long it takes before it is time for Mr. Santorini's third-grade class to get our turn in the library. I love the library because it smells like old books, which is not a gross and dusty smell but the pretty smell other people's hands leave behind when they flip pages of books they love. And because there is a corner where I sit when I make my book selection each week and it is cozy and I could stay there all afternoon reading, especially if it is an Amber Brown since Amber Brown just seems like someone who would do handstands with Elinor and me all afternoon (and then worry about third grade with *just* me all evening). But mostly I love the library because Mrs. Noone — whose name makes me think of noon, as in lunch, and as in a bright and cheerful break smack in the middle of a long school day — is the librarian. She helps me find books that I will like even if they don't have Amber Brown in them. (As in, she knows I will read just about anything that has to do with the stars and the moon and astronauts.)

"Who are you going to choose, Jules?" Elinor asks after Mrs. Noone gives us all kinds of books to look at. "So far I like

Amelia Earhart and the Queen of England, or maybe Serena Williams," she says. She sounds so excited.

"Oooh, the Queen of England is a good one," Charlotte says. This sounds like a compliment, which makes me very suspicious. "Let me know if you don't choose her."

"Okay," Elinor says, looking at me and crinkling her eyebrows. I shrug back. "I'm probably not going to choose her. That would be too obvious."

"Well, I'm going with da Vinci," Teddy says.

"Da Vinci the artist?" Charlotte asks.

"Yep," he says.

"The one who painted the *Mona Lisa*?" she asks.

"Yes," he says.

"You, Teddy Lichtenstein, are choosing an artist?" she asks. "I don't get it." There's the old Charlotte.

"He was a scientist, Stinkytown. What's to get?" Teddy shakes his head at her and puts his hands out like Big Henry does when he hand-talks like a grown-up. And Elinor and I burst out laughing because he actually called her Stinkytown to her face and it is very funny, but I also feel kind of terrible about it.

"My name is Pinkerton, Charlotte Pinkerton," she says, and now this reminds all of us of Mr. Santorini calling us all by our last names first and we all burst out laughing, even Charlotte, until Mrs. Bright-as-the-Sunshine-at-Noone comes over to shush us.

"Have you decided, Jules?" she asks.

"Amber Brown?" I ask, squinting. I'm getting so used to squinting, I forget I'm doing it.

"Has to be a real person," she says. "Maybe Judy Garland or Katharine Hepburn for you," she says. "Old-fashioned Hollywood actresses!" Her eyes get wide when she says this, and even though those ladies sound very interesting and important, when I look at their biographies, I just don't think they're very me. And this makes me think that actresses are something else. Something glamorous and elegant and talented — talented in a different way than the cast of *Look at Us Now!* Talented like the people who hold up trophies on awards shows and say lovely things in speeches. I think if I were ever talented like that, and someone decided to give me an award for it, I'd probably trip up the stairs and then forget what I was going to say when I got to the microphone.

I shake my head at her.

"Well, selections need to be in by Friday, and then you'll have two more weeks to do your research, make your timeline, and design your costumes," she says. "Come to me if you need more ideas." I look around at Teddy, who is bursting with excitement over da Vinci; at Elinor, who likes so many different people she's practically jumping up and down; and at Charlotte, who probably knows exactly who she will choose and

★ 89 ★

who will probably have the absolutely best costume, since her mom is an actual costume designer. I go from feeling very excited to feeling very lost. Right now, I wish I had the writers from *Look at Us Now!* working for me. Then, in parentheses, the script would say, *(Jules chooses _____)* and I would know exactly what to do next.

# gummy shoes, doctors without orders, and sitcom-y solutions

By the time the end of the day comes, my head is so tired from thinking about the wax museum and my eyes are so tired from fake-squinting that I think I might need a doctor for real, which is a good thing, since that's where we're going.

The good news is, the rain has gone away and it has turned into a cooler day. I am excited to be wearing a corduroy skirt (finally!) with argyle tights and turquoise rain boots. There are even some leaves blowing up around us and I feel like fall is on its way. I zip up while we wait for the bus.

I tell my mom all about the wax museum and the rap and she asks who I'm going to be.

I shrug.

"Want me to help you think of someone?" she asks.

"Maybe," I say, but I want to change the subject. The bus comes just in time. "Will there be shots?" I ask my mom once we're seated.

"I honestly don't know," she says.

I stare out the window feeling nervous and wondering why I pushed for a doctor's appointment anyway. I mean, I have to miss *Look at Us Now!* rehearsal. But then I picture Charlotte and her polka-dot glasses and I remember. She just looks so different and so smart and so . . . different. I picture myself walking into school tomorrow with glasses — Turquoise with stripes? Argyle, like my favorite socks? — and I feel like squealing. Between that and the wax museum, this really would be the best school year ever. I almost forget all about the possible shots until I picture a nurse coming at me with a big smile and a syringe. I feel my knees start to shake, so I try to distract myself with a list.

*The Good Things About Missing Rehearsal:*

1. I was so frustrated yesterday I thought I might explode, so a little tiny shot might be better than a full-body explosion.

2. I still don't know how to be a ventriloquist's dummy since acting like a real dummy means acting like a doll and not like a human person and I barely know

how to act like a human person
in the first place.

3. Big Henry got his playdate after
   all. He went home with a new
   kindergarten friend named
   Marco, which means that he is
   not here to drive me crazy and
   it also means that he has a
   friend.

We hop off the bus and head down the
street to the doctor's office. I play a game of
dodging all the black gum marks on the
sidewalk and think about how the mayor
once went on TV to tell everyone not to toss
their gum on the sidewalk and now every

time I look at those marks I think that it was gum and that it was once inside someone's mouth and so I absolutely cannot touch even the sole of my shoe to something that was once inside someone else's mouth.

And right after they weigh me, and measure me, and check my reflexes with the rubber hammer, the big moment arrives.

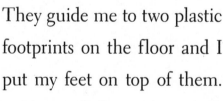

They guide me to two plastic footprints on the floor and I put my feet on top of them. I say a little prayer inside my head before I look up from my feet. *Please let the letters be blurry. Pretty, pretty please.*

"Let's go, Julesie," my mom says. "Show off your twenty-twenty vision."

I look at the chart while my mom goes on and on to the nurse about how we come from a long line of perfect vision. No glasses in sight. Ha, ha, ha. My stomach drops down to the footprints on the floor. The letters aren't even a little bit blurry. I think for one whole minute about pretending I can't see them just so I can go shopping for glasses with my mom and without Big Henry, and just so I can make that big entrance at school. But as I stare at the big *E*, I know I can't. I know I will never need glasses, and I know this means third grade will never be as perfect as I wanted it to be.

My perfect vision and I wake up early and go back to the not-perfect third grade. At school, we spend the morning in the library during our scheduled time and we get to look at more books to decide who we want to be. The thing that has me mad is that the people who already know who they're going to be get to start their research, which means Teddy, for one, has a very big head start. We have two more days to decide and then it has to be approved by the third-grade teachers in case the person isn't appropriate or in case you chose the same person as someone else. Apparently, two Sacagaweas is one Sacagawea too many.

Teddy is hard at work on his da Vinci project and I am feeling very jealous that he is so excited. I don't feel that way about anyone I read about. I mean, I like the Helen Keller story, but I'm definitely not a good enough actress to play her; and I really like Florence Nightingale because her life was very exciting, but then I picture all that blood and sickness and my head starts to spin; and then I think I might like to be Teddy Roosevelt, since my dad is OBSESSED with Teddy Roosevelt and always makes us stop and look up at the big statue of him on his horse at the Museum of Natural History. But I don't think I'm a good enough actress to be a man. I can't even be a ventriloquist's dummy.

"How about Eleanor Roosevelt, then?" Elinor asks.

"Who's that?" I ask.

"She's the one with the statue in Riverside Park," Elinor says. "Plus, her name's Eleanor!"

"Teddy Roosevelt was her uncle," Teddy says.

"How do you know these things?" I ask.

"Why do you think my name is Teddy?" he asks.

"Wow," Elinor says. "Are you a Roosevelt?" she asks.

"I'm a Lichtenstein," he says, and we all laugh. "But we're big fans of the Roosevelts. And Eleanor Roosevelt did a lot of interesting things, according to her statue in the park, but she wasn't a mathematician like da Vinci, and a scientist and an artist and a physicist, and —"

"We aren't listening anymore, Teddy." It's Charlotte and her glasses talking. And I want to be annoyed with both her and the glasses for talking this way to Teddy, since I am the only one who is really allowed to talk to Teddy this way, but then I remember that he called her Stinkytown this week, so he kind of deserved it.

"Who are you choosing, Charlotte?" I ask, realizing that she has been very, very private, which means she's up to something.

"Not telling you, Jules. You'll just steal it."

"I will not," I say.

"Yes, you will, because it's the best one to do," she says.

Elinor and I look at each other and say at the same exact time, "Who?!!"

"Jinx," Teddy says, never looking up from his pile of da Vinci books. And we are all quiet for a good, long time after that.

Mr. Santorini comes over to us after a while and says, "How's it going, kiddos?"

I feel stuck, because I really shouldn't talk since Teddy never released me from the jinx, but I SHOULD answer my teacher. I look at Teddy, who is deep in his book now and not paying attention. I think he forgot about the jinx!

"Going that well, huh?" he asks again.

"It's going well, Mr. Santorini," Charlotte the unjinxed says now. "There are so many people to choose from!"

Elinor and I look at each other and I watch her give Teddy a little push to remind him.

"Hey, no pushing!" he says, before realizing that Mr. Santorini is standing there watching.

"No pushing is right, Elinor," he says. "That's a yellow for a warning." I gasp out loud since I don't even care about the jinx anymore now that Elinor has gotten punished for something Teddy did!

Elinor's face twists up a little, so when we line up to go back to class I grab her hand. "Are you okay?" I ask, but she just shrugs in a way that looks like tears are coming, and the one thing I absolutely can't watch is a crying Elinor. The only other time I saw her cry was when she told me about her summer with her dad and how her parents were actually getting divorced — DIVORCED! And I just didn't want her to ever feel that sad and I hate feeling like there isn't any way to make someone feel better.

"Don't cry," I say. "Yellow isn't that bad."

"What's worse?" she says.

I think for a second. "Red!"

She smiles. "I was just trying to get Teddy to say our names three times," she says.

"Did you hear that, Teddy?" I say. "You got Elinor in trouble."

"I think I might throw up," he says. Teddy always thinks he's going to throw up when he gets nervous, which is why it is VERY hard to stay mad at him. "I just forgot. I was reading about da Vinci and I forgot!"

I look at Elinor and realize that I want her to forgive Teddy so he doesn't actually throw up. That would make everything much worse.

"It's fine," she says, but she doesn't look fine, and I see her staring at the yellow flag on her name for the rest of the day. I wish she would just go over to Mr. Santorini and explain the jinx so he would turn her back to green, but she doesn't. And she doesn't participate at all, which she always does because she's so smart and confident and always raises her hand. I am so mad at Mr. Santorini. If there's one person in the entire world who should never, ever get a bad-behavior flag it is Elinor.

At the end of the day, we walk out together and I ask if she's going to tell her mom.

"That's the thing," she says. "If I tell her,

she'll probably tell my dad, and I don't want him to think I'm doing a bad job in school. I was kind of hoping he'd even come to the wax museum."

"Tell her that," I say. "And maybe she'll let you have an almost-invisible lie just this once."

"What's that?" she asks, smiling.

"It's the kind of lie that doesn't hurt anyone, and it can even help people," I say, thinking of how I got the hug from my mom on the first day and that helped me and it didn't hurt Big Henry NOT to know about it.

"Thanks! We'll see what she says. But I like it!" She seems happy for the first time since the yellow flag, so I am very relieved.

I just wish I could make her parents' divorce invisible.

In the car service on the way to rehearsal, I ask my mom why she's never told me about this da Vinci guy, since she's an artist and everything.

"Oooh, Leonardo da Vinci was really something, Jules. He was a little bit of everything."

"Seems like he was a lot of everything," I say, thinking about all those things Teddy was saying about him.

"Yes, I guess he really was. He's what you call a Renaissance man. Is that who Teddy chose?"

"How'd you know?" I asked.

"Because he's kind of a lot of everything, too," she says. "I think da Vinci's a great choice for him."

I think about Teddy and his nervous throw-up face and I shake my head. "Teddy Lichtenstein, Renaissance Man," I say seriously, in my TV-voiceover voice, and my mom and Big Henry and I all laugh. It's a funny thought.

"I want a playdate," Big Henry says.

"You had a playdate yesterday," I say. "With your new friend Marco, remember?"

"Stop talking like I'm a baby," Big Henry says.

"Hank!" my mom says.

"You *are* still kind of baby," I say. Then

my little baby brother kicks the seat in front of him just as we get to the studio, and my mom hustles him into the babysitting room while I go find my sitcom family.

Jordana and John McCarthy come running over with excited faces.

"What? No glasses?" John McCarthy asks.

"Nope," I say. "Just my plain old face. No glasses."

"Your face is not plain," Jordana says. "Are you bummed out?" she asks with her Southern drawl. She sounds so nice when she talks. And this reminds me of Elinor and her nice accent and her love of sports and how those are her things. And then I think of Charlotte and her pink polka-dot glasses and her big opinions and how all of that is her thing, and then I think of Teddy and his smart brain and how that's his thing, and all of this makes me feel that lost feeling I had in the library after the wax museum announcement.

Plain old lost.

"You know," John McCarthy says, "on sitcoms there's always a solution to every problem, and the solution always happens within twenty-two minutes." I love having a sitcom big brother. I wish I had a real-life big brother who would say very smart things all the time.

Jordana stares at him. "You know, John McCarthy, you're right," and when she says *right* it sounds like this: *raaaaght*. "What if we ask the writers to give Sylvie glasses?"

"Is that possible?" I ask, suddenly very excited.

"Maybe, baby," Jordana says. And all I can think as we march ourselves over to the writers' table is that I want a sweatshirt that says *I Heart Jordana*.

When we get to the table, the writers don't look up. They always have their noses in a script and they are always drinking coffee, and it is not the tall-icy kind of coffee. It is the piping-hot kind with little hand protectors on the cup. It could be one million degrees outside but writers would drink piping-hot hand-protector coffee no matter what.

"Sorry, kids. No can do on the glasses this season, but maybe we'll think about it for next season if all goes well."

"If all goes well" reminds me that *Look at Us Now!* will be on TV this Sunday night and that there will be a party and that people will be watching me be Sylvie and that they might hate it. Or maybe they'll love that first episode, the one where I dance on the counter, and they'll love the next ones, too. They'll love them all up until they get to the ventriloquist's dummy episode.

I feel those knots forming — the orange-Swish knots, the dancing-on-the-counter knots, the mudslide-in-Canada knots — and I know I have to find some way to figure this out. I only have two more nights before

I have to choose the perfect wax museum person, and I only have two more nights to get this whole ventriloquist's-dummy thing right before taping or else all will not go well and none of us will have jobs next season and Sylvie will never, ever get glasses.

TAKE SEVEN

## colorful behavior, the drama of the eight-year-old, and a good time to bring up tubers

I wake up and I am still mad about Elinor's yellow flag. Still mad at Mr. Lamb-and-Peppers Santorini, who is no fun and doesn't think anything's funny and who thinks jumping jacks are a good idea right after you've eaten hot chicken and rice at lunchtime.

"Why so stormy?" my dad asks. I almost act even more stormy when he asks this but then I think of Elinor and remember that I am happy to see my dad when I wake up every morning and happy that he cares if I am stormy.

I give him a hug.

"MUCH better," he says. "Wow. Did you see that, Big Henry? That deserves a pancake."

"Will it have flaxseed in it?" I ask, squinting. Not a hoping-for-glasses squint, but a hoping-there's-no-flaxseed-in-my-pancakes squint.

"Yep," he says. I groan. "And chocolate chips."

"Yes!" Big Henry and Mommy say at the same time.

"Jinx!" I say. But then I release them right away and get back to being mad at my very mean teacher.

"Who are you going to choose for the wax museum?" my dad asks.

"There's no one just right. I don't have a thing," I say.

"A thing?" my dad asks.

"Like you have cooking," I say. "And Mommy has art, and Teddy has science, and Elinor has sports and being English."

"You have acting," he says.

"But not the kind of acting they like for school projects," I say.

"Why don't you tell your teacher the problem and see if he can help?" my mom says.

"No way, José," I say, then I tell them the whole story of yesterday to make them understand.

"Why didn't anyone explain the situation to him?" my mom asks. "That's where you need to use your voice."

I eat my pancakes and think about this. I picture myself with an old-fashioned megaphone screaming "WE WERE JINXED!"

at Mr. Santorini. "What if he gives me a yel-low flag for using my voice?" I ask.

"He won't," my dad says.

"He might," I say.

"Not if you're polite," my mom says. "I promise."

"I wish I had a script for life," I say. "I would do so much better at it."

"We all wish that," my mom says.

"But parents always know exactly the right thing. I feel like you did get a script." My mom and dad smile at each other.

JINXED!!!

"Um, no," my dad says. "Thankfully, you only remember the good things we say."

"So far," my mom says.

"Time for school!" Big Henry says, shoving some Legos and stuffed animals into a bulging backpack.

"You can't bring all of that to school," I say.

"I want to use it in sharing time," he says.

I feel mad at him for having sharing time with Ms. Kim when I have to go face that cuckoo Mr. Santorini and his Hawaiian shirt and his completely and totally unfair behavior chart. I give him a little extra push out the door, which I'm glad my mom doesn't notice.

Today at library time, I feel mad from the second I walk in, especially when I see Charlotte and her glasses with her nose in a biography of Julie Andrews. This reminds me of second grade, when Charlotte was trying to be bossy Maria von Trapp in the moving-up play, and now I'm thinking, *Oh, so she's going to be Maria von Trapp and isn't that just perfect?*

"Jules, I've got it!" Elinor says. Of course she's got it.

"Who?" I say, but I kind of don't want to know.

Everyone has someone perfect to be except for me.

"I'm going to be Jackie Robinson," she

says. "He's a baseball player — a very important one."

"He?"

"Yep," she says.

"Perfect!" I say. She is the exact person who could do a boy character as a girl, which makes me jealous, so I'm kind of acting but Elinor doesn't know this. Almost-invisible lie number three.

I flip through pages and pages of people who did lots of interesting things but none of them have anything to do with me — they have to do with baseball and science and history and it all sounds very serious and important. I stop for a minute at Elvis Presley and imagine my dad singing "Teddy Bear" into his spatula, and then I think of myself dressed up as Elvis in *Jailhouse Rock*, with jail clothes on and a guitar. And when people push my wax museum button, which will be made out of a soda-bottle cap and painted silver, I will say in a slow Southern accent, "I'm Elvis, ma'am, the King of Rock 'n' Roll."

I think my dad would be proud of this and I think it would be fun to slick my hair and wear a jail jumpsuit. I can kind of picture myself doing it well, maybe even really well — the same way I can actually picture myself playing the dummy really well. I'm just so afraid to try. I put away the Elvis book and put a Post-it inside my brain for when Big Henry does the wax museum. He'd be a perfect Elvis. He'd probably be a break-dancing Elvis, which would make the best wax museum biography ever, and he would be famous because that's just Hank — he's likable and entertains people without even thinking too much about it. Having things be easy is his thing, I think.

"Elvis?" Charlotte says, laughing.

"I'm not being Elvis. I was just looking," I say.

"I think you should," she says. "I think Elvis would be perfect."

I feel my heart start pounding because I think Charlotte is making fun of me or something.

"It would be so funny with your hair slicked back and a big funny suit and a stand-up microphone." And now she's laughing, and so are Elinor and Teddy, and I just feel like everyone's making fun of me.

"Why don't YOU be Elvis, Charlotte! You're the girl with the big, loud voice about everything. You be him. You'd be better at being him than you would at being Julie Andrews!" Then Charlotte runs out of the library and Elinor and Teddy are staring at me.

"Jules," Mr. Santorini says, and I know before I even turn around that he is shaking his head and that head-shaking is the thing that comes right before a yellow flag. This is the what-if I've been dreading.

I decide to use my voice. "Did you know that tubers are really just root vegetables, like potatoes?"

He squints at me, but I go on. "Could be a white potato or a sweet potato, or maybe a radish —"

"Jules, why is Charlotte crying in the hallway?"

I shrug.

"You have no idea? You don't think it has anything to do with you yelling at her?"

How did he see me yelling at her but not her making fun of me? It's the same way he saw Elinor push Teddy but did not see that we had been jinxed by Teddy in the first place. I really think *he* might need glasses! I feel that popping-popcorn feeling in me and I want to run into the hallway, too.

I know I have to use my voice to say what happened since he didn't SEE what happened, so I do. I let it all out. I tell him that all the jumping jacks he has us do make me nervous, that the behavior chart makes me even more nervous, that Elinor was only trying to get Teddy to release the jinx, that Charlotte was making fun of me, that she always gets everything, and that everyone has a thing except for me. I tell him all of those things and I say them fast in case he stops me with a Captain von Trapp whistle he's been hiding in his Hawaiian shirt. I would not be surprised.

I am afraid to look over at Elinor because I have the feeling she will be mad that I brought up her yellow flag all over again since she likes to handle things on her own. And now I'm wishing I hadn't said anything since Teddy could get in trouble for jinxing us. But I don't even know if that's possible because I don't understand the rules of the behavior chart in the first place. I feel a little dizzy.

"Sounds like we need to step outside," he says.

"For jumping jacks?" I say. But he doesn't say anything to this and I know from my

own parents that when they don't say anything, they are really mad.

We pass by Charlotte, who has Mrs.
Noone helping her wipe her nose, so while
she's with the sunshiny librarian I'm with
Captain Cuckoo.

I go out into the cool air and this is the
first time in two weeks I'm trying *not* to
squint — squinting will squeeze out the
tears that are burning in my eyes. "Let's try
and figure this one out without jumping
jacks," Mr. Santorini says. I am relieved at
this news and suck in some air.

"I have a question," he says.

"You do?" I ask. I keep thinking he's just
going to tell me to race him or something,

so it is confusing me that he's acting like a regular teacher.

"Why would you bring up tubers at a time like that?"

I snort at this. I forgot all about the tubers. I can't believe he's asking me about tubers at a time like this. I think for a second. "I thought it was interesting, and I thought it was something Sylvie, my character, might do that would get a lot of laughs."

"I understand you're an actress," he says. I nod a little because it always sounds funny when people say I'm an actress since I still don't feel like an actress. "So, I would have thought an actress would have a big, loud voice and lots to say about everything. And here you've been quiet as a mouse since the first day of school."

"Am I allowed to answer?"

"Of course!" he says. "My classroom is a place for lots of questions. Lots of everything." *It is?*

"I'm afraid of the behavior chart." I close my eyes tight as soon as I say it.

"It's nothing to be afraid of," he says. "It's just there to make sure we're all checking ourselves."

"But I never know what's going to get me in trouble, so I'm afraid of doing anything."

"Something tells me that if you just act like yourself, you're not going to have any trouble with the behavior chart. I think it's probably the NOT acting like yourself that has gotten you into trouble today. And what's the trouble with Charlotte?" he asks.

I tell him how she was making fun of me for wanting to be Elvis and how I didn't even want to be Elvis and then it felt like everyone was laughing at me and how it feels weird that everyone but me has the perfect person for the wax museum. I also tell him that I was jealous of her glasses, and I haven't even told my mom that. And then I tell him how I don't know how to be a dummy and that Big Henry is probably the physical comedian they are looking for on *Look at Us Now!* Now I've told him two things I've never told anyone else!

"And John McCarthy says on sitcom TV everything can be solved in twenty-two minutes and I just really want this to be like sitcom TV, I guess. I'm frustrated," I say.

"That's because it's frustrating stuff. But I'm going to think about this one and you're going to apologize to Charlotte because

I think you hurt her feelings and that is something Jules Bloom being herself would not do."

I nod. "Am I getting a yellow flag?"

He looks at me for a good, long time. "Not today."

I let out all the breath I think I've been holding in since the first day of school. And then we get on with the day.

After school, I tell my mom to wait before we get in the car to go to rehearsal. I see Charlotte and I walk over to say sorry.

"I wasn't laughing at you," she says.

"You were," I say, and now I wish I hadn't come over. This is what happens when I am

Jules as myself. I get mad and frustrated and I don't know the right things to say.

"Well, you have everyone calling me Stinkytown," she says.

"Not everyone," I say. "Just Teddy. And I'm sorry about that."

"You'd be a good Elvis," she says. "You're an actress. A good actress." I can't believe she just said that.

"You'd be a good Julie Andrews," I say.

"No," she says. "I won't. I can't be a good anyone."

"What?" Who is this Charlotte and what has she done with the other Charlotte?

"It's the glasses. No world-famous people have glasses! Except maybe the Queen of England and even Elinor doesn't want to be the Queen of England. And I can't believe you're having any trouble at all." Her voice is getting loud. "You get to not wear glasses, Jules. You get to be Elvis if you want — you get to be ANYONE you want, but not me. I have to wear glasses all the time and Shirley Temple did NOT wear glasses, and Julie Andrews did NOT wear glasses, so no matter what, I won't look like them, and you know you're just so LUCKY."

She is yelling and for the first time I realize that Charlotte did not get glasses just so she could make an entrance.

"You don't like the glasses?" I ask.

"I hate them!"

I start to laugh. "Why are you always laughing at me?" she asks, still yelling.

"Because all I've ever wanted is glasses and you got them and they have polka dots and I even went to the doctor to try and get glasses and I even asked the show writers to give Sylvie glasses and you hate them!"

"Really?" she asks.

"Really," I say, and I see my mom waving at me from the car. "I have to go. I'll come up with a solution. There's a sitcom solution to everything."

"Who says?"

"My big brother," I say. "And big brothers know everything."

TAKE EIGHT

## breakfast for dinner, made-for-TV brothers, and favorite things

We were supposed to tape the show tomorrow and I was supposed to miss a whole afternoon of school, but all because of me, we are not taping the show tomorrow. And all because of me, we are having another rehearsal tomorrow so I can get the dummy just right. And all because of me, we have to tape the show on a weekend! This weekend — the same weekend as the *Look at Us Now!* premiere party.

When we get home, my mom stops me and tells me to knock. I am in a very frustrated mood and just want her to open the door already.

"Do it," she says.

I knock.

Someone knocks back.

I knock again and look at my mom. She shrugs.

Someone knocks back. I am about to knock back when I hear, "Say 'Who's there?' already!" from the other side of the door.

"Who's there already?!" I say loud. And I

hear Big Henry crack up on the other side.

The door opens, and Grandma Gilda is standing there like a present with a big bow on her.

"You said the next time I had a prank I should do it in person!" We hug and hug and I am so happy. And so hungry!

We have breakfast for dinner and Big Henry is sitting next to me gobbling up his scrambled eggs and toast and he is chewing too loud and it's making me nauseous. I growl at him.

"AAAAAAH!" he yells. "I hate Jules!"

"What?" my mom asks, looking at Grandma Gilda and me and not at him. "Calm down, Hank," she says, trying to go near him for a hug. But he flails at her and screams some more. "I don't want to go to kindergarten and I don't want to go to sitcom practice and I don't want to do homework and my tooth is WIGGLY!"

I feel my eyes get very wide and I feel a little bit like I want to laugh. But I just don't do anything. I watch as my little brother throws himself on the floor and kicks and screams at the top of his lungs, and then he just starts crying and then the front door opens and my dad walks in and all of a sudden I feel like crying, too.

My dad walks over and sits down on the floor next to where Big Henry is lying flat on his back and we all just stay on the floor for a while. "What's going on?" he asks.

"I think that kindergarten is a bigger adjustment for Hank than we realized," my mom says.

"But he makes it look so easy," I say.

"That's his thing," my dad says, rubbing Big Henry's lying-on-the-floor head. Then we sit there for a long time until my mom says, "Well, maybe we should paint something on the wall."

At this, Big Henry finally sits up. I try not to be grossed out by the snot coming out of his nose and his sweaty head. I take his hand. Big Henry is not known for his tan-trums. He is known for saying funny things and wearing rain boots when it isn't rain-ing. This makes me feel lost all over again so I hold on to him tightly.

"Paint something like what?" I ask. "Are we naming something?"

"Let's write what we want instead of what we don't want," she says, coming out of her pantry/studio with a can of paint. It's a light blue, since the last time we did this the paint was red and it was very hard to paint over it. "Positive affirmations," she says, smiling at George.

"I want to go back to nursery school," Big Henry says.

"I want to go back to second grade," I say.

"I want to go back to Florida," Grandma Gilda says. Then Big Henry just cracks right up like he does — the crying-and-laughing-at-the-same-time kind of crying.

After a while I put him to bed myself, and I read to him and I don't make him try to read even one word. I pretend like he's in nursery school.

The next morning when I get to school, two things are different:

1. There is a brown paper package on my desk (tied up with string!) just like the song in The Sound

of Music. Written right on the
on the package, it says:
Inspiration. Please stay behind
at recess. Those two things do
not go together in my head.

2. There is a new name on the
   behavior chart and it is not a
   new student. It says Mr.
   Santorini, and he has a yellow
   flag already!

We all can't wait for him to start class so
we can find out why he gave himself a
yellow flag. When he does, he says, "I realized that it wasn't fair for all of you to be
accountable for your behavior if I am not

accountable." I have no idea what *accountable* means, but it sounds like it means if we have to be afraid of the chart, he should be afraid of it, too, which means I love the word *accountable*.

I raise my hand for the first time this year and he calls on me right away. "Why did you give yourself a yellow flag?"

"Great question, Jules. Because the other day, I was a little too quick with a decision to give out a yellow flag. Some things need explaining. I should have taken a minute to find out the facts."

I look over at Elinor, who is smiling ear to ear, and then I look at Teddy, who looks now like he might throw up from relief! I tap my pencil and bounce my knee all morning, waiting to open that package, and then I race through lunch — salad bar! — to get to recess.

"Aren't you coming?" Elinor asks when we line up.

"I don't think so," I say, looking around. Then the assistant teacher tells me to go back to the classroom, and Elinor looks worried. "It's a good thing," I say, and then I hurry off toward my brown paper package.

When I get to the classroom, Mr. Santorini has a laptop computer all set up. I open up my package then and it's a DVD called *The Best of I Love Lucy*. "May I?" he asks. I give him the DVD and together we watch just about the funniest show I have ever seen.

Whoever this Lucy is, she's what people are talking about when they say *talented*.

I watch her get into trouble in a chocolate factory, and she's busy stuffing chocolates in her mouth to keep up with a conveyor belt and I start to laugh so hard my shoulders are shaking and Mr. Santorini is laughing right next to me.

"Who is this?" I ask. "Why are we watching this?"

"She's Lucille Ball, and she was one of the great comic actresses of all time and she's extremely interesting."

"I love her!" I say. "I love Lucy!" I look at my teacher. My new favorite teacher. "For the wax museum?" I ask.

He nods. Then he kind of squints at me. "And for your show?" he asks. "It sounds like you have a case of the what-ifs."

I wrinkle my nose at him.

"Like what if you really go for it and be the dummy the way you know you can and then it isn't good enough?" he says.

"Or what if it isn't as funny as I mean it to be?" I add.

"So, yes, what if that happens? And what if I had given you that yellow card after all?"

I shrug and I realize that I don't even know what would have happened and that's what scares me.

"I think you're afraid of not knowing how things will turn out, and I think the reason Lucy is a good one for you is that I think she was the kind of person who threw her fear right into her work and that's why her work was so good. She didn't just pop those chocolates into her mouth and hope we all laugh at her, she made her eyes pop out, she stuffed them into her shirt, she went for it. Really went for it. And generally speaking, in life, when you go for it — all in — you almost always get a lot out of it."

I've been nodding ever since he started talking and all of a sudden I can't wait for rehearsal. "I think you solved my problem," I say.

"I'm good at solving problems when you talk to me."

I walk over to the behavior chart. "May I?" I ask. He nods.

Then I turn his yellow flag back to green, where it belongs.

"Do you want to come to our premiere party on Sunday night? Ms. Kaplan will be there," I say.

"I would love to, sailor," he says. "You know, you've missed recess."

"I know," I say. And I know what's coming.

"Ten-hut!" he yells. We do jumping jacks together until the class comes back and I have all kinds of energy for the rest of the day.

The energy lasts all the way to rehearsal, which Grandma Gilda takes me to. When I tell her all about Lucille Ball, she goes crazy!

"Of course, Lucille Ball," she says. "This Mr. Santorini knows a thing or two."

"You're kind of like Lucille Ball, you know," I say.

"I know, I've been told that before," she says. "But so are you. People either have comedy or they don't. You can't teach it to them."

This time, I decide to get that dummy just right. I get it. I picture Lucy's big old eyes and her worried expression and I know I'm about to go all in, like Mr. Santorini said. Something in me just clicks, and as the scene goes on, I can hear Grandma Gilda laughing all the way from the fake stage they have set up for Spencer and Sylvie's performance. Her laugh gives me that same kind of energy those jumping jacks gave me, and I decide to take a chance toward the end of the scene when Spencer says "Knock-knock" to Sylvie as the dummy. I knock on his head. He clears his throat and tries again. "Knock-knock." I knock on his head again. Spencer looks at the director.

I think he wants to stick with the script. But the director gives the rolling sign and we continue. "You're supposed to say 'Who's there?', Dummy," he says.

"Who's there, Dummy?" I say. And then I bet they could hear Grandma Gilda all the way on the Upper West Side when she laughed. Thank you, Lucille Ball; thank you, Mr. Santorini; and thank you, George.

TAKE NINE

# deep breaths, pushy reviewers, and coming attractions

My mom comes with me to tape the ventriloquist episode, and then I change for the party and give big hugs to my sitcom siblings. Everyone has their own party to go to.

"This is kind of it, isn't it?" I ask my mom in the car.

"Kind of what?" she says.

"Either people are going to like the show or they aren't," I say.

"Yep," she says. "And some will like it and some won't. And some will like *The Spy in the Attic* and some won't," she says.

"Mmm-hmm," I say.

"And you will get to decide if you like acting enough to go through all of that."

"I do," I say. "I love it."

"I love you," she says. It's like she has that mom script again. The perfect mom script.

We pull up to BLOOM and it looks beautiful, like it always does, and my dad has put a CLOSED FOR A PRIVATE PARTY sign in the window. All of my friends are there and all of my parents' friends and Ms. Kaplan and

Mr. Santorini and Uncle Michael and the whole rest of my family from everywhere. And there is a big buffet of Mother's-Day-brunch-type items.

The show's about to start. Everything is perfect except Elinor is sitting alone in the corner. "Are you mad at me because I told Mr. Santorini about the jinx?" I ask.

"No," she says. "I'm mad that my dad's not coming to the wax museum."

"Did your mom tell him about the yellow? Is that why?"

"No," she says. "She liked the invisible-lie idea."

I smile.

"He just has to work and it's a long way to come for a silly school project and he'll try to come soon." She says this with a final big breath in and out, and I think this means she doesn't want to talk about it anymore.

I realize that this is one of those things that cannot be solved in twenty-two minutes.

"Will you sit next to me to watch?"

"Yes!" she says.

"And will you tell me the honest truth, even if you hate it?"

"Yes," she says.

"Pinkie swear?" I say.

And we do.

Then the lights dim and we turn on the TV and then I can't believe I'm sitting there watching a TV show that I'm in. I really can't believe it. And everyone is laughing

a lot, and giving me pushes during the
commercials — not the kind of pushing
you do when you need someone to release
a jinx, the kind of pushing you do when

you can't believe something. You just really
can't believe it.

Afterward, I grab Teddy and Elinor and
we march over to Charlotte the way Jordana

and John McCarthy and I marched over to the writers: as a team.

"I can solve your problem in twenty-two minutes," I say to Charlotte.

"How?" she says.

"Just don't wear the glasses for the wax museum. You made it all the way to third grade without them. What's the worst thing that could happen?"

"She could run into a wall," Elinor says.

"It'll be a scientific experiment. Very da Vinci."

"Or very Lucille Ball," I say, and we laugh.

"Really?" Charlotte says. "You think I could do that?"

"Yes! It'll be fun," I say.

"Like a sitcom," Charlotte says.

"Like a sitcom," I say.

Then we eat all kinds of desserts and act out the whole wax museum, taking turns pretending to be Charlotte without glasses until we practically fall down laughing.

Finally, everyone is gone and we close up BLOOM and head home. We walk by a newsstand and Big Henry grabs my coat and screams my name. "Jules!" he yells at the top of his lungs again.

"What?!" I yell back. The new kindergarten Big Henry is VERY demanding.

But when I turn around he's holding up a magazine, and Emma Saxony, the teenage megastar, is on the cover, and peeking out

from a small box in the corner is a picture of me, Jules Bloom — Bloom, Jules — and it says: *The Next Big Thing?*

I stare at it and my mouth hangs open.

I hear my mom and dad and I definitely hear Grandma Gilda.

"Eddie," she says. "They got it just right, except for one thing."

"What?" I say.

"There shouldn't be a question mark on that picture," she says. "That editor should be fired."

"What about me?" Big Henry asks.

I put my arm around my little brother. "You're already a big thing, Henry," I say.

"See that?" my dad says. "No script necessary." I smile.

Then we walk past a man blasting some rap music from a boom box and Big Henry just starts break-dancing, right there on the street. I get embarrassed for exactly one second before I shrug my shoulders and join him.

# ACKNOWLEDGMENTS

A whole lot of people helped Jules make it all the way to her third grade debut. Starting with Jill Grinberg, whose support of Jules from day one was the best gift any writer could ask for. And Jenne Abramowitz for being Jules's best after-school tutor and her constant cheerleader — with tremendous support from the one and only Abby McAden.

To my incredible family — from my husband and kiddos all the way up to their aunts and uncles and crazy-supportive grandparents!

Jules was brought to life in pen and ink and gouache by the marvelous Anne Keenan Higgins and her stylish imagination — many thanks, Anne!

And then there are these friends — the rooting kind of friends who last well beyond third grade and those who — okay, maybe I didn't *know* in third grade, but it sure feels like it. Without you — Rhonda Seidman, Denise Goldman, Alisa Schindler, Randi Goodman, Amy Flisser, Kim Lichtenstein, Lindsey Allen, Stacey Kaufman, Stephanie Bhagat, Marion

Rosenbaum, Leigh Richards, Laura McMillan, and Diana Berrent — procrastinating would be a lot less fun!

A special thank-you to the inspired third-grade teachers at Manorhaven Elementary School — because of Dr. Brevig, Mr. O'Brien, and Ms. Haut, I got to experience the Wax Museum from the inside out. Your creativity and dedication is remarkable — what a lucky bunch of kids!

To the real Ms. Kim, kindergarten teacher extraordinaire, and the real Mrs. Noone — you really do light up the place, and we all know how you light up our kids and their reading eyes. Thank you!

As always, many thanks to The Dolphin Bookshop and especially Vivian Moy.

Finally, to my kids' friends, who make me laugh and think really hard, thank you most of all.

# BETH AIN  was raised in Allentown, PA, but fell in love with New York City first as a little girl after hot pretzels from a corner stand warmed her up on a cold winter day, and again later, right after she knocked the mirror off of a city bus with her U-Haul the day she moved in. The driver quickly forgave her and she quickly decided it was the greatest city on earth. She did eventually head for the hills of Port Washington, Long Island, where small-town life has no shortage of inspiration, and where she can see the Empire State Building on her morning run — making it pretty easy to imagine what Jules is up to over there.